Oksy, Come Home

A Blood Scouts Novella

PHIL WILLIAMS

MMXXIII

ISBN-13: 978-1-913468-28-6

Cover design by P. Williams

Published by Rumian Publishing

Visit **www.phil-williams.co.uk** online for more information and regular news regarding the writing of Phil Williams.
Join the newsletter to be the first to hear about new projects.

1

Dearest Okselle,

I am not sure if this letter will find you, or in what condition. Hopefully you are far from trouble, though it's rather late to expect that of you now. We have not heard from you since Relight, but I have told your brother not to fret. Things were always at their calmest, after all, when you had no news to report.

I was inspired to write to you today because I saw Mr Patterswald in the market. He is well. The town has generally moved on. Things, indeed, are quite settled here. Perhaps it is time you came home?

Studying the communications building through her scope, Oksy was acutely aware of how conspicuously weak the defences looked. Most of the violence-churned environments she'd crouched and crawled through during her six weeks on the front line had been reinforced with sandbags, scraps of metal, razor wire and traps. This squat white-washed brick building, a cube two storeys high dotted with square windows, sat untouched by gunfire or bombs, and unadorned by obvious defences.

"Hubris, ain't it," Corporal Wils Hold, her sniper companion, decided. He was a lanky, bird-nosed youth, maybe a few months older than Oksy, maybe slightly younger, who claimed to be the best marksman in 4th Brigade. She'd accompanied him on three missions now, including a twenty-hour period in a tower with fantastic visibility over straggling enemy troops, and she could confirm he was a middling shot at best. At least, by her standards. But he was senior on account of enlisting four months earlier than her, and on account of not being a woman, so he got to hold the rifle while she only had a scope with no weapon to attach it to.

Damned if Oksy was going to let a lack of equipment restrict her, though. Even if she couldn't shoot, she was more observant than Hold. She had identified this as the headquarters for the men responsible for the Drail's Dagger Legion. And less than a mile from the front line, there was a reason they were in this innocuous building and not somewhere more fortified.

"See them up there." Hold peered through the scope of his rifle, perched on the ground. They were prone under the broken shell of a partially collapsed vehicle shelter, hidden but at a lower position than Oksy would've liked. There wasn't much else around, though; the fighting had moved through here less than a month ago, leaving wall fragments where buildings once stood. All except that white building, where Oksy followed Hold's gaze to an upstairs window, two men silhouetted inside. They were lit from behind, nothing covering the window. Hold went on, "We're far from the fight. They found an undamaged place, took it for their own, thinking it was safe, and now they're strutting about with no idea we got ways of getting this close."

Oksy didn't give him a response, considering it *might* be possible but still looking for imperfections. Her father had always said the simplest things could surprise you. Was there a stray wire attached to explosives? A shimmer that might betray touched metal, capable of alerting earth-minded mages? Anything that could suggest a trap? She scanned the corner of the building and along the base, over the rubble. There was a lot of rubble; that was odd. The building sat isolated, untouched, but bits of broken brick and paving ran right up to its edges. The ground had been unsettled, only the building itself stood unharmed.

"What, then?" Hold said impatiently. "Come on out with it. Think it's a mirage? Or they got snipers in some invisible high spot? Because I don't see no towers around. Just some pompous bloody Drail officer waiting to get his head popped."

Oksy lowered her scope and considered the scene as a whole again. Invisible defences, that was the game, wasn't it? They'd come this far by keeping well out of sight, and their success depended on striking essentially unseen themselves. The prize was right there: two officers moving past the windows, ripe for assassination. They might get a couple more if they were lucky, before retreating into the shadows. But the enemy could hide, too . . .

"You scared or something?" Hold grumbled. "We'll be out of here before they can say snapboggle, right? Confirm the distance, wind, I'm doing it."

"What's your dad do, Wils?" Oksy asked, scoping the broken roads around the building. Her companion gave an inarticulate grunt of confusion so she went on, fully intending her questions to slow him down. "Back home, what's your dad's job? Is it something he'd like you to follow in?"

"Butcher, isn't he. Yeah, it's steady work I might get into. What of it?"

"My dad was a town planner. He worked on our town's central committee, solving problems for a whole community. Spent every day trying to come up with creative solutions to complex problems. He's always encouraged me to look beyond the obvious. The more you know, the more opportunities present themselves. The problem you need to address might not be the one you think you need to."

"Are you giving me a bloody lecture right now? This is why no one talks to you, Oksy."

"I'm *saying* we need to think about this differently. Besides a gunman in a tower and the plainly absent battle defences, how else might a command building be protected?"

"There's no sign of parsing magic. And Dagger Legion ain't got a mage, we know that."

"We *think* we know that," Oksy corrected. "Though I agree, there's no apparent magic at play here. Nothing in the air." That and shield barriers were hard to maintain for any length of time; very unlikely when the enemy had no reason to suspect a threat. "But there are other things that can stay hidden."

"Sure, the road might be mined, but we ain't going closer so who cares?" Hold replied.

"Or there might be a daraszk nest in the cracks. Or toxic fiend-weeds on the roof."

"What the fuck's a darak?" Hold snorted. Oksy wasn't going to teach him about the vile hornets native to this region, which everyone should've been aware of already. She didn't see any tell-tale signs of staining on the walls and most wildlife had been driven off by the fighting or poisoned by gas. Likewise fiend-weeds, which could emit an awful poison if disturbed, weren't reliable enough for the Drail to use as a defence. But the point was there were other possibilities.

And there it was, a small chink of rubble moved in the road. About halfway between their position and the headquarters door.

"A *zemnihobot,*" Oksy whispered, voice quietening with awe. "Very rare."

"Are you making shit up again?"

Oksy raised an eyebrow. In the weeks they'd known each other, many of their conversations had ended with Hold's unwavering decision that Oksy was trying to trick him, mostly because he had a limited vocabulary. Granted, she'd embellished a few harmless details here and there, but on the whole she didn't have to – the man simply didn't know much. He just assumed that he knew more than *her,* so when she brought up something unfamiliar she had to be lying. She'd hoped to get away from these kinds of bickering mind-games when she left the girls back home to join the military. She usually got on better with men, and the soldiers had been mostly considerate and welcoming in Laine's Brigade. Before she'd been sent on to Wayflower's and paired with this resentful weasel.

"It's a creature found in eastern Garter," Oksy explained. "Better known as the land kraken?"

Hold mugged at her, waiting for a punchline. She offered her most neutral, light smile, to invite him to look for himself. He shook his head, then checked the building, looked back to her, back to the building. He demanded, *"Where?"*

"That's the point," Oksy sighed, and shifted a little closer, to guide his rifle with her hand. "Zemnihobot are great at hiding. Even better at rendering a territory utterly impenetrable. There was a guild of Garter moneylenders who spent decades training each one to defend the most valuable locations. The sort of place so wealthy it might come under siege. See that." She'd only just picked it out whilst talking, but sure enough the sign was there: the lock and wing symbol of a bank, faded and worn above the building's double-door entrance. "This must've been one of those buildings. The Dagger Legion commanders came here for a reason."

"What the hell are you talking about?" Hold growled. "No such thing as land kraken, that's a story they tell kids to keep them from trespassing on abandoned property."

"It's there," Oksy said. "This road hasn't been damaged by bombs, or the building itself would show the signs. It's been unsettled by the beast underneath. Zemnihobot are clever, though. They drag debris back over them, pat it down. The best-trained ones can preserve the building at their centre, leaving the surrounding area fully functional except when they're specifically triggered."

"And how the hell you know all this?"

"I told you, my dad worked in town planning. It pays to know what the world is up to."

Hold blew out an irritated breath and gave up his disbelief. "Well so what then? Even if there's something under there, it won't move faster than a bullet. We can plug those nobs and high-tail it out of here."

"No, we can't," Oksy said. "Land kraken are big, Wils. It might stretch two hundred yards out. Might be under us right now."

Hold glared at the ground as though it'd just offended him.

"We should head back, report in. They could send someone better equipped to deal with it. Or fire over some artillery."

"Took us two days to get here," Hold said. "They could be gone by the time we get back. *If* we get back. And if Wayflower had artillery he wouldn't be sending us out all over, would he? I didn't crawl all this way out here for nothing. Screw it, I'm taking the shot – if it's really something there, and you're not just pissing with me, then it'll focus on the men screaming inside, not us, won't it?"

"Trained zemnihobot don't work like that."

"We'll see, won't we? And we can outrun some underground squid. Give me the distance."

Oksy held in her immediate response, that he was being an idiot, and paused to consider their chances. They were probably just outside the reach of the land kraken, and might escape it, but it was a big risk. There was an alternative. She thought of her father's 'monster' manuals, as she'd called them as a child. Books spread out across the grubby living room floor, documenting all the wonders of the world. Her mother had always complained she should be playing dress up with the neighbourhood girls rather than reading that disgusting nonsense.

Oksy told Hold, "Zemnihobot have a weakness which was pretty unexploitable ten years ago. Maybe not now." Oksy considered their rifle. A wooden-framed Long 0.48. One of the most accurate and powerful rifles in the Stanclif Empire. "When alerted, part of the land kraken's head surfaces to take in a full sense of the surrounding area. It's a target about two feet wide, with a nerve centre in the middle, maybe fist-sized? We shoot that, we could kill it. Or incapacitate it, at least."

Hold kept staring through his scope, brow folded hard as if focusing enough might give him a better handle on the situation. A better idea than her. She imagined he wanted to ask again just how the hell she knew all this, but instead he said, "Then what?"

"Then Dagger Legion's command have no other serious defences. They'll be forced to relocate. We can pick off a few more as we retreat, or get word back quickly enough for a squad to follow up, catch them on the move. The point is, we'd flush them out."

"By shooting a giant squid in the head."

"Well, it's not quite that simple. It's not its head exactly – it's a small target, and if we miss we unleash hell."

"I ain't gonna miss a giant squid."

"No but you need to hit its nerve centre. Fist-sized, remember?" Granted, she'd embellished that bit about the exact size, to heighten how important accuracy was, but she imagined it would be small.

"Do *you* want to take the shot?" Hold spat. She narrowed her eyes, trying to decide if he was serious or not: doubt hidden under his surface anger?

She volunteered, "To be safe, I do have the steadier hand. Faster reflexes."

"You bloody *what?*"

"I graduated top of the class at Killen's Estate. I had the highest average of –"

"I don't care how well you did in bloody *class*. I'm senior here. You're just a damn spotter. A girl one, at that." Hold shook his head in exaggerated disbelief. "Highest average my cock. I'll show you how it's done."

"We only get one chance at this, are you –"

"I said it, didn't I?" He went back to his scope. "Second window in. That's an officer there. I'll pop his head, then when your kraken shows up I'll do him and all. Where are we expecting it?"

"I don't know. It could show anywhere around the building," Oksy admitted, not adding *that's why her quicker reflexes would be useful*. "Probably near the main entrance. In their training, the bank staff would –"

"Alright. Distance and wind."

Oksy bit down her deep desire to take over. Do a better job. She took a breath and lifted her scope again, checked the measurements. Land kraken or not, Hold was right about one thing: the officer in the window *was* an easy, arrogant target. She gave Hold her readings, then said, "I really think I should do it."

"I really think you should shut up," he replied, adjusting the scope. Shoulders tight, he clenched his teeth, barely steadied his hands and pulled the trigger.

The 0.48 boomed through the ruins as the window shattered and the officer dropped.

Something much bigger and more ferocious boomed back, even louder.

The ground exploded around the building entrance and the world quaked underneath them as a shape shot up, slick brownish red and speckled with glassy, blinking orbs that may or may not have been eyes. Hold brought the rifle down, took rapid aim and fired again. The brickwork erupted a foot to the side of the probing monstrosity. A miss. A second later, as Hold racked the bolt, the appendage was gone. He fired again anyway, putting a bullet through the door, and this gunshot was met by the thunder of the ground exploding to their left.

Oksy dived out of cover, braced to run as Hold swore loudly.

A giant, reaching tentacle tore out from the earth towards them.

2

I do not say this to be glib or dismissive, but the more time that passes, the more we are all quite sure you overreacted. Your brother insists you were unaware of the full implications, but we both know you're too bright for that. I suppose you merely hoped to get a stronger reaction. I understand, though, you made it a point of honour, and you have always had a weakness for pride.

However, you could not have known, surely, the extremities of the conditions you were leaving us for. I am sure you have seen it all well enough now, and might at last change your mind. This is not a thing to be stubborn over.

Oksy thumped herself down at the end of an empty table, as far from the growing crowd of soldiers as she could get. The mess hall (actually a big tent) was half full, noisy with bustling men and heady with the mixed stench of stew and sweat. She slumped over her tin bowl and stared into the lumpy green dinner, finding now that she'd settled she wasn't sure she had the energy to lift her spoon. The gloop was hardly appetising, and was probably barely nutritious – she wouldn't be missing much if she just left it and fell asleep on the bench.

Its grimy, viscous texture was also way too familiar to zemnihobot slobber.

It'd been a long journey back, hiding in pipes and ditches, and she was happy to return to a company of strangers. No obligation to talk to anyone. Back in Laine's Brigade, half the men would've tried to spark a conversation by now. Since she'd been transferred to Wayflower's, barely a fortnight ago, she'd mostly just been getting ugly looks, not too dissimilar to back home. She hadn't yet had the time, or energy, to pick out guys worth introducing herself to, and Hold hadn't helped by pointedly slinking away from her every time they returned to base, like he was ashamed to be seen with her. Every time before now, that was. At their final parting, he had been reaching for her, screaming desperately for help, as a thick tentacle constricted his body and dragged him towards a writhing patch of earth.

She was unsure if being here without him would make things easier or harder.

"Join you?" a guy with a rough Stanish accent asked, sitting down before she had a chance to look up. He was skinny with a narrow head, his unruly mop of ginger hair regrown in an all-too-typical mess since its complete shearing at recruitment. No one much cared about their hair once soldiers had that first buzz. Oksy hadn't even received that much attention; she'd been rushed through so quickly she'd avoided a haircut altogether, and her hair was now longer than ever. She'd let it down, coming into the mess hall, to hang conspicuously over her shoulders, giving it some much-needed air.

"Any good?" the man said, nodding at the stew. He had a plate of his own, and rather than wait for an answer tried a big spoonful. Oksy watched a familiar show play out: a contortion of sudden, alarmed disgust, eyes bulging and lips pursing. A careful, painful attempt to force himself on, chewing slowly, then a swallow, with a little inhale for fresh air, and a look of blessed relief. He concluded, quietly, "I've had worse."

Despite the reaction, he went in for another spoon, this time going through the tableaux quicker. He sped up and by the fourth spoon managed an almost genuine smile, convincing himself it wasn't so bad. He paused then and said, "Toothless Baze, they call me."

Oksy assessed him briefly with a slightly cocked head, appreciating that despite his thin frame, which made his loose grey-blue fatigues appear especially bulky, and his gritty tone (from the Normul region, she suspected), he had smooth skin, a good sharp nose, plump lips. When he smiled again she noted "Toothless" also had a set of straight teeth, whiter than most. She gave him a questioning look.

"Ain't on account of my appearance," he said. "You know what the lads are like."

The lads in question were starting to fill up more of the tables and some of the discussion fell away in favour of scowling at Toothless for sparking up a conversation with the one woman there. Probably the only woman in the barracks. They weren't jealous looks, but disapproving ones.

"But listen," Toothless went on, setting himself firmer on the bench, arms close to his sides. "We noticed you ain't been about recently, must've had a tough job? I know this lot ain't been too welcoming so far. I figured it about time someone reached out. I'm dying to know how it is you got here. And, I guess, kind of, what it is you do?"

"What I do?" Oksy echoed. They all knew she was partnered with Hold, obviously a marksman. But she wouldn't be surprised if they had seen her as some kind of especially daring assistant. A little coldly, she said, "I shoot straighter than anyone in this brigade."

The young man averted his eyes with a nervous laugh. "Okay. You're a lot prettier than anyone else, too, you know that? Should be some kind of crime, I reckon, setting someone pretty as you out here." Worry suddenly crossed his face, as if he'd surprised himself. "I'm not trying to hit on your or make things weird. I got a sweetheart back home. That was just a factual observation, understand?"

"Got it."

"My point being, how's someone so pretty get to be out here?"

"Same way as everyone else, more or less. I wanted to do my bit to protect our homeland." He waited, holding her gaze, so she went on, citing word for word what her father had told her: "We let the Drail go unchecked in any one of the fifteen regions they've expanded into and it's a chink that could one day damn us all."

"Uh-huh, but you could help out by working back home, right?"

Oksy rolled her eyes. She'd been through this as many times as she'd met someone new in this war. But it was a distraction. If she closed her eyes she'd only see that thrashing kraken, hear Hold's final crunching cry. Some conversation was better than none. She said, "All the girls in my town were marching into the factories. Doing work that doesn't require a brain. I wanted to do more than pack boxes or sew clothes. I wanted to make an actual difference.

Something I could see. I wanted to learn new skills. Get a change of scenery. All the same reasons as you, I guess?"

"Sure." Toothless stifled another laugh. "Right. I wish I was in a factory. I got called up. And got a family back home that needs the money, so why not. Made it an obvious choice, or not really a choice at all. It's what we're good for, all us blokes, so they say. A woman, though? Fighting and all? I ain't judging just . . . doesn't seem so obvious?"

Oksy watched his face, checking for a jibe, or a backhanded sentiment. No, he genuinely seemed interested. She said, "Anyone can use a gun, not just –"

A couple more men rattled the table and interrupted with huffs as they sat down on the benches near them. The room was almost full now, cutlery and bowls clattering, voices rising. One of the newcomers grumbled, "Hell you talking to her for, Tooth?"

Oksy leant a little closer to Toothless, over the table, to finish her point: "Firing a gun's as easy for me as any man. I figured I could be at least as effective as the next man."

Toothless looked apprehensively amused, but the newcomers twisted in their seats to stare at her. The one who'd spoken wore an ugly grimace, like she'd just spat in his food. She lifted her spoon to finally eat. The stew was lumpy and excessively salty, but not too bad. The man shook his head and turned his back on her, grumbling a curse she chose not to hear. This was more the attention she was used to.

"You must be good at it," Toothless continued, more quietly. "Shooting?"

"I don't like to brag," Oksy said, and left him to draw his own conclusions. The way her dad had taught her. It took Toothless a second, then he laughed – briefly. Something caught his eye and he abruptly stiffened, eyes down on the stew.

Oksy frowned, glancing sideways at the other men, expecting them to have put him off, but they were looking down, too, and she noticed a general quiet sweeping the room as someone walked in. Oksy lifted a leg over the bench to turn and sighed with disappointment, not sharing the other soldiers' fear, as she saw their brigade commander, Colonel Wayflower, stomping through the crowd. A bottom-heavy man, wider around the waist and legs than up top, he had a small head, a stiff, pompous walk, a sharply pressed blue uniform and a self-important feathered cap. His slits of eyes were aimed right at her. Trailing behind him was a stumbling, officious-looking moustached aide.

Oksy stood and stepped out from the table, into the small open space at the rear of the tent, as the colonel clomped between the tables, soldiers darting out of his way. Oksy refused to blink as Wayflower got closer. She had quickly got his measure when she'd been transferred: a poser, given this command because his family were big in the mining industry. He sold himself as a *thinker,* a strategist, but Oksy was well aware of the unimportance of this particular stretch of the front line he had been assigned to, and the general tactics here to simply hold the line. The fighting might still be brutal but advances wouldn't contribute much to the movements of the army at large; if Wayflower had true value as a commander, he wouldn't be here.

She suspected he knew that well enough himself, and his insecurity led him to making reckless decisions in an attempt to impress, such as sending their limited number of scouts out on unnecessarily dangerous assassination tasks. He'd also never hidden his dislike for having a woman assigned to his command, having barely let her speak on arrival and done nothing to properly equip or apply her.

"Private Price, how long have you been back in camp?" Wayflower demanded, stamping his feet together as he reached her. He tilted his head back, to look down his nose at her.

"I came straight here, sir," Oksy answered, aware of how quiet the rest of the mess hall had become. "I thought –"

"Was it not part of your orders that you debrief the *moment* you return?"

Oksy knew better than to say the first thing that popped to mind, especially when dealing with supposed superiors. Part of her had forgotten her duties altogether as she traipsed back into friendly territory, but she may also have semi-consciously avoided going in to report. She'd spent a day and night putting distance between herself and the land kraken – she was in no hurry to relive the memory. She said, "Yes, sir."

"And you lost Corporal Hold?"

"I didn't lose him, sir," Oksy said. "But he's not coming back." And there it was, the images returning, those grasping tentacles, chunks of rubble erupting around the kraken's snapping maw as Hold was stuffed into it. She suppressed a shudder, and instead refocused on the colonel's question. "You already heard, sir?"

"Word tends to spread fast when you unleash a savage *monster*. Were you just hoping we wouldn't find out how massively you messed up?"

"I was going to report in full," Oksy said, stiffening. "I just needed to catch my breath. We did what you asked –"

"You *compromised* our infiltration efforts. You alerted the Drail we had scouts in the area and have single-handedly managed to increase their security along the border ten fold. We lost another squad caught in the shuffle, did you know that? No, of course not. And that's the tip of it."

"I didn't even have a gun!" The cry came out unbidden, his escalating tone grating hard against her. Oksy had failed to keep calm with the entire mess hall watching her public reprimand. Only Toothless appeared sympathetic instead of entertained, but he averted his worried eyes.

"Do you know," the colonel said, "precisely how many able sharpshooters we have in the Stanclif military?"

"Not precisely," Oksy admitted, and under his mean gaze (expecting a humble *no?*) she chose to elaborate. "In terms of specifically trained marksmen, I know we had a couple of dozen around the start of year, and two emerging schools I'm aware of – my own training took about six weeks, and we had eighteen graduate in that time, so if we assume five or six –" She paused, aware Wayflower's face was darkening, and quickly finished. "Maybe fifty or so able marksmen across the Empire. Factoring in casualties."

"Forty-seven active!" the colonel spat out righteously, as though she'd answered entirely wrong. "It was forty-eight before you lost Hold."

Oksy resisted the urge to repeat she hadn't lost Hold, and waited to see where this punishment was going. He wanted to make an example of her, to take some blame for the collected Drail efforts that had made their lives so difficult. Never mind that the lack of marksmen was precisely why he needed her, or that she'd done exactly what had been asked.

"I told them you were a mistake. That we didn't want you here. General Macwest can keep his blasted experiments with alternative soldiers. You've not only cost us a valuable asset, but have reinforced the Drail's position at the same damn time."

"Sir, if you'd let me report in full?" Oksy came in, carefully. If she could just get a calm word in. Disastrous as their attack had turned out, she and Hold had surveyed the secure sites in a couple of miles' radius, at least; it would be easier to locate the Dagger command next time. She'd thought this through on the way back: they wouldn't use the bank anymore, now the land kraken was exposed. They'd either be in a metal silo she'd located, or a Cane Saints church; it was valuable reconnaissance. "I believe I know where we can find –"

"Quiet!" Wayflower swept on over her. "It's plain enough what happened. You distracted our sniper, got him killed and failed to harm any significant Drail leadership. In fact, you made such a noticeable mess of it that we can now expect" – he hissed the next part, a hint of relish creeping through his malice – "an enemy mage to reinforce their efforts here. A dirt-minder, no less, is reported to be en route from Sand."

A rush of upset comments went through the crowd and Wayflower's crusty lips tightened with satisfaction as he kept his eyes on Oksy. She stared back, impassive despite feeling the collective disappointment, and blame, of her fellow soldiers. This was tired and familiar. They wouldn't care that Hold got himself killed; that the Dagger command were already well-protected; that the approaching mage was probably on his way before any of this happened. None of that mattered if Wayflower could transfer everyone's frustration onto her.

"Private Price," the colonel continued, as the hubbub died down, "understand that it's taking a good measure of my will not to merely have you shot. You wished to be a soldier, to play at a man's game, so you deserve strict punishment. But I, at least, believe in the principles of Civilisation, and of women's honour. You will be reassigned according to your apparent ambitions. Report to the 203rd Infantry, at Jaggo Point, by dawn."

Oksy translated it in her head: the higher-ups probably wouldn't let him dismiss her outright, and it wouldn't do to be seen punishing a woman, so he was sending her somewhere terrible. Her brow knitted as she tried to process the number, the position. Then the name clicked. "In the trenches?"

"The vanguard," Wayflower corrected, with a smile that said it was a truly unwelcome honour. "Under Captain Caracker."

The name was met by hushed comments from their audience, even a few satisified laughs. Caracker was apparently well known. Not a good assignment, obviously. And Oksy was well aware of the danger of being on the very front of the front line, rather than hovering back and forth about it. The men who filled the trenches were little better than human shields for the Empire's land. She answered quietly, "Will I get a gun there, at least?"

Wayflower sneered, disgusted by the mere suggestion. "If Caracker has any sense he'll give you an armful of bandages and have you sing to the wounded."

The growing whispers bit at Oksy as much as her condescending commander and she bit back more firmly than she intended: "I'm not a nurse. I'm trained as a sniper. I learnt from Major Heskeph – I was one of the best shots in my training corps. I can out-shoot any man here."

"You will do exactly as you are ordered!" Wayflower cut in, suddenly booming, chilling Oksy and every solider in hearing-distance into silence. His eyes suddenly shimmered with instability, lower lip quivering as he continued. "Insubordinate. Arrogant. You were sent to me as a *joke*. An insult. But I will not stand for it."

"I wasn't –" Oksy started, but he cut her off again.

"Enough! Not another word." The man was deranged, nerves hanging on by a thread. Too vain about his command to realise Oksy would be a boon to any sensible leader. She wasn't going to convince Wayflower of that, though. Same way she hadn't convinced Hold. All she could do was meet his eye and strain to hold down the defiance in her eyes.

Her best hope was the same as always, she supposed. Carry on.

Prove them wrong.

"When you report to Captain Caracker," the colonel concluded, with grim finality, "I will advise that he take a very firm hand with you. Try not to die." Those last words said as if he intended for the exact opposite.

3

You must appreciate your mistake now. We all make them. You were never good at accepting that, though; you are such a smart young thing, you are used to being right. Perhaps that's your father's fault for coddling you. He never understood that even special children need boundaries.

No one will judge you for this, though. It is okay to be wrong. You do not need to be there – it is a place for rough types and brigands. Not someone as delicate as you.

Captain Caracker was an ogre.

Not a figurative ogre, but an actual, eight-foot-tall brute, the width of two men, limbs thick as a human torso, face wide and creased with deep, malicious lines. Oksy paused as she crouched into his command dugout, a cavity in the earth barely big enough for a regular person, let alone this hulking monster. She had seen a couple of ogres in the Stanclif ranks since joining the army, but never up close. They weren't a common species, nor generally welcome back home. He almost totally filled the space, his table for maps and correspondence and a cupboard for supplies pressed up against the walls. He sat on a chair made invisible by his bulk. Even seated, he was stooped, glaring at her. His uniform was only vaguely Stanclif blue, a patchwork of different outfits customised to accommodate him, chest in a vest lined with stuffed pockets, hard-muscled arms sleeveless.

"Private Oksy Price," Oksy announced, tightening her pack against her shoulder. "Reporting for duty."

The world shook around them, bits of ground tumbling from the ceiling, and Oksy consciously dropped her centre of gravity to avoid stumbling. The rolling thunder of a large weapon followed, then a series of incomprehensible shouts, from various directions. Soldiers were rapidly moving through the trenches, and a patter of footsteps passed behind Oksy. The whole time, Caracker didn't move, but kept glowering at her. He had a mug in one head-sized fist, gently steaming. She was supposed to be afraid, obviously, but she returned his look with more fascination than fear, until the commotion died down and he growled, "So you're the one got Hold killed?"

His voice was deep and scratchy, exactly how she'd expect an animated boulder to sound. His appearance wasn't far off, too. And she was gripped by the strength of the malice he directed at her; the realisation that Wayflower hadn't just sent her here because Caracker was a hard-arse. Oksy said, with growing caution, "You knew him?"

"Knew him? I owed him a blood oath."

"Oh."

"Right, oh." The ogre straightened up, the unseen chair creaking painfully under him. "You know what an ogre blood oath is?"

"Well, yes," Oksy replied. More than that, she suddenly also knew Wayflower was expecting Caracker to deal with her in a way he was too pompous to do himself. Meaning at the very least right now she had to talk her way into buying some time. "Blood oaths are actually quite common over a variety of cultures and species – the tradition adopted by the Azrian howling vengers is particularly interesting – but in times of war, such oaths have widely been accepted to become more transient; given how frequently lives are saved and lost during battle, the honour comes in continuing to fight for the same cause, with leniency for the specifics."

The ogre's face took on a very un-ogrish expression at her rapid talking, somewhere between bemused and disgusted. Surprised, either way. Caracker said, slowly, "Think you know a few things, huh?"

"I read a lot, sir. My father always told me that feeding curiosity is one of the best investments anyone can make with their time."

"Your daddy ever give you a book by someone that weren't a human?" Before Oksy could reply, *yes, actually,* he went on, "Ogre codes of honour ain't made for loopholes. That boy saved my life once, and I swore him protection. You've made me a black-hand.

A defaulter. Me and probably a thousand others who owed him."

"I disagree." Oksy hurried on. "Meaning no disrespect, Hold wasn't very pleasant and he wasn't a very good shot – it was *not* my fault he died. If he'd been willing to give me a chance, I could've completed our mission and he'd still be alive. We could've saved more lives. He actually *cost* lives, if you think about it."

The ogre's relatively small eyes glistened like black beads as his cheeks reddened at her gall. "You usually have trouble keeping your mouth shut?"

"Only when I feel like I have something important to contribute, sir."

"The man's bloody well dead. I oughta break your skull in two, talking like that, maybe repay the debt that way."

Oksy took a breath. But ogres respected strength more than anything, she knew that. She said, "You'd be making the same mistake he made. Thinking I don't know how to fight."

His arms flexed and he rose slightly. Oksy darted back into the doorway. Her hand found the hunting knife strapped at her thigh, to rest on the handle, and Caracker paused.

"What kind of girl are you?" he snarled. "Gonna pull a knife on an ogre?"

"If you make me." Oksy tried to keep her voice steady, but her adrenaline was building up, body itching to move: fight or run. "I'm fast and I'm accurate. And I know your skin is thick, but the way your arteries bulge, it's actually *easier* to make an ogre bleed."

As his coiled muscles threatened to launch at her, a short barrage of gunshots sounded nearby, more shouts echoing down the trenches. Oksy glanced sideways, unsure if the noise was something to be worried about or just a regular day down here. When her gaze fell worriedly back on the ogre, she found him staring thoughtfully.

"You ain't convincing me you're smart, no matter how many books you've read," he rumbled, "but you got some guts. Might count for something. Leave off the bloody knife. Enough young 'uns dying in this war already that I ain't got any mind to hurt our own. Especially not a woman."

"I can fight," Oksy assured him again, bitterness creeping out even as he gave her a reprise.

"Yeah, I almost believe it. You've got a sturdier frame than most human waifs, I'll give you that. Sure you're not part ogre?"

The comment threw her, and Oksy released the knife, straightening up again, more self-conscious now. She'd long ago made her peace with not being a slim girl, even on military rations, but wasn't sure she liked being compared to an ogre.

"First time on the front line?" Caracker resettled his considerable weight with a fresh squeak from the dying chair.

"Not exactly," Oksy said. "I've been taking up positions up and down the line for over a month now. I've crossed into enemy territory three times."

"But usually you're in some tidy hideout. Safe and away from the action."

Oksy let her silence admit it. She'd be lying if she said mastering the science of staying hidden wasn't one of the biggest appeals in specialising in marksmanship. This was a war where just to be seen was likely to get you killed.

"Well, the trick here is simple: keep your head down. There's only a hundred metres separating us from the Drail. They're cowering in their trenches, we're cowering in ours, and any day or night someone might start up a ruckus. We stay here, they stay there, we occasionally take a nip, or give a nip. We move, we die."

"Okay," Oksy replied warily. He almost sounded friendly, imparting this advice.

"I ain't gonna mess you up, like Wayflower wanted," Caracker went on, apparently reading her expression. "Fact I couldn't keep Hold safe is my burden to bear, and I expect you're right. That prick might've lasted longer if he were willing to ask for help. You . . . Well, fuck it, you're here now. And didn't even come armed. Find the quartermaster and get a rifle. Then find yourself a spot and settle in. Shoot any green-coats you spot but otherwise stay out of trouble until I say otherwise. At some point they'll fling us all up over the top."

Oksy swallowed; she appreciated the chance, but less so the hopelessness. For all her training and smarts, he wanted her to sit still and wait to join a charge of bodies? Everyone knew how well that had worked out at the Battle of the Basin.

"Something more you want to say?" Caracker said.

"Yes, sir. I can hit a man with pinpoint accuracy at two hundred metres. Just give me the right weapon and a target. It's a waste, putting me here."

"And I can break men apart with my bare hands but I'm trapped in this ditch, too. I have to crawl to make it from my bed to the shitter. You don't like this, it's your own fucking fault for signing up. Ain't some princess picnic party. But you know what, I give the boys hope, looking big and nasty like I do. Maybe you'll give them some hope too, if you're as good as you claim. Long as they're not too focused on those big tits."

Oksy shuffled to tighten her arms in a way that might better hide her chest. Even though it wasn't at all visible through the baggy uniform anyway.

"That'll be all, Private. I've got a drink going cold here." He held up his mug demonstratively and the steam wafted out towards her. Oksy picked up a scent of cocoa and orange, some sweet spice. Cinnamon? "Dismissed."

Oksy wanted to argue – after a rocky start, the ogre *was* reasonable. His expression warned her against staying, though. She lightly saluted and turned away. Maybe she would have better luck with the quartermaster. With the right gun, she could make something work down here.

"Price," Caracker called out, unnecessarily loud so his voice rumbled past her. She saw a couple of soldiers huddled down the trench look up and clock her. Oksy turned back, forcing a smile. "I *know* Hold was an arsehole. He was still one of my boys. And so are you, now. Survive long enough and I'll make up my own mind how useful you are."

Oksy frowned, not quite a vote of confidence, but it wasn't too far off. She might be okay. Other than the lurking threat of constant death. She nodded and ducked out along the trench. The channel was seven feet deep so she didn't have to stoop, but it was hard to resist that urge when the open air above meant death. Her boots splashed through mud where the ground wasn't fully boarded, and she smiled at the first soldiers she had to squeeze past. Grubby-faced and weary, they gave her uncertain looks in return.

After almost an hour of clambering about through the maze of narrow pathways, carefully avoiding stepping on people and generally keeping her head down, she finally located the quartermaster, a long way back and trying to organise barrels being lowered from above. He barely looked at her as he gave her a basic mumbler rifle from a stack of them, a weapon whose simple production and reliable function had changed the face of the war. It was not fit for her abilities. She asked if he had a Bowstown Long or a Hallwood 0.42 and he gave her an impatient stare, saying nothing until she left.

Oksy spent another hour learning the lay of the trenches, this time introducing herself to occasional soldiers who smiled back with courteous nods or shook their heads in some kind of summary judgement. She finally found a dugout to set down her pack on an unoccupied cot, one of eight narrow planks rammed into the clay walls of the man-made cave adjoining the trench. Two soldiers were crouched there, taking a break from keeping watch. They welcomed her and introduced themselves, too tired and distracted by a general vague malaise to even note she was a woman. They offered her stale bread and a warm mug of a thin liquid that pretended to be soup, then said if she didn't have specific orders she might as well join them on the next shift. One said, "It's basically like sitting in here, waiting, except we do it out there."

Happy to idle in the meantime, Oksy took out her book and tried to read in the dim light of a single candle. Her current read was a history of 5th-century Remland traders and pirates. She'd got through one page when a roaring shout sent the trenches into turmoil.

"Mindless!" a man cried, his voice getting louder as he drew closer, repeating it as he ran. "They've got a mindless!"

Oksy and the two soldiers hurried out into the trench, guns ready, scanning up and down as other soldiers emerged from their holes and jumped up alert, as if there was anything they could do.

"Mindless!" the shout continued, sweeping down the line.

Oksy wanted to know exactly where this news had come from, and why with such a sense of immediate panic? They had known, after all, an enemy earth-minder was on the way. Even if someone had spotted the mindless mage, getting everyone worked up wasn't going to help. Then a shadow fell over the trench and she looked up, with a hundred other soldiers, to see something monstrously large falling from the sky. Men yelled and shoved at each other pressing to get out of the way, but there was no space to get by and nowhere to go. Oksy was shoved hard into the slatted mud wall, the breath knocked out of her, and someone trod on her foot as he passed. She shoved back, just to get some space, then squeezed herself small rather than join the throng. The falling object looked like part of a building.

It was exactly that, she realised, just before impact – the corner segment of a great brick structure, easily ten metres across. She crouched, one arm up uselessly as it came down, about to crush them all – but the collision came just above them. The huge object smashed apart against an invisible barrier that shimmered vaguely blue. With a great series of cracks and thuds, the building segment scattered overhead, parts of it thrown off in all directions, and the fleeing soldiers started a new chorus of screams and redirected as the trench was hit by a rain of masonry.

Oksy backtracked into her dugout, and watched a particularly large segment of wall thump down into the trench – right on top of the men she'd been talking to – embedding itself in the earth.

Behind the shouting up and down the line, she heard far-off laughter, chillingly loud and wild, surely from the enemy trenches.

The Drail mage Wayflower had promised. Someone who could tear up parts of the world to toss right on top of them. He might send tremors through the trenches themselves, or help the enemy build a tunnel. A mage like that was a weapon more powerful than all their troops combined.

But the attack hadn't entirely succeeded, breaking up before crushing the trench entirely. Her Stanclif leaders must've found a mage of their own, Oksy realised: only a parsing witlacer could produce a barrier like that. It was an incredible feat, one that must've saved many lives, even if the crumbling bricks still cost a few. Her new roommates included. It was also likely to have drained the defensive mage, though from the sound of his manic laughter the Drail's mage was weakened, too.

Oksy slumped down on her cot, finding her hands were shaking, heart beating fast. She stared at the great chunk of building now blocking her exit, all but trapping her in. Liquid seeped around its base, maybe muddy water, maybe blood. Men's arms came clawing at the sides, spades chipping in, the troops hurrying to start repairs. But Oksy just stared. Being in danger, in combat, wasn't getting easier, no matter how she told herself calmness would save her. And the injustice of it only made it worse. The Drail had one person with a particular skill that could change everything.

She was one person with a particular skill who could do the same.

If only they'd let her.

4

Day by day, I hear more awful stories of the young men from town. Young Junny Vils has returned to us missing two legs and one arm. Can you imagine? And Win McBride, I have heard, that irascible boy you wasted last summer with, he was killed in some anonymous field in Lome. By a grekkel, if you can imagine! It is bad enough for the men to endure. I would prefer anything but that for you.

Things here are never perfect, but it is your home. Did you truly think so little of the life we made for you? What of your future? Your studies, the Conservatory? You are an intelligent woman, for heaven's sake, Okselle. I don't understand how they even allowed you to enlist.

After her dramatic start to life in the trenches, Oksy found the following fortnight dragged by with little event. The Drail earth-minder was apparently satisfied with the chaos caused by dropping half a building across their lines, and had been silent since. Biding their time, building up energy or forming a plan. Maybe just operating in some other area. Whatever the case, Oksy itched to crawl over the wire and find the mage herself, to preempt another attack. She was sure she could find him easily enough; if he was in the area, he *had* to be either in that silo, about a mile directly north of Jaggo Point itself, or the church a half-mile or so to the west. But on the one brief occasion she'd suggested it to Caracker, he snarled her off, saying they didn't have the manpower to spare crossing the line, nor the support from Command to do it.

In fact, they barely even let Oksy poke her head up to watch the broken field that separated the two sides, leaving that duty to *more experienced* soldiers. Besides sitting up against the trench wall listening for the enemy, ready to jump in if someone got shot nearby or Drail soldiers randomly appeared, Oksy's duties were consigned to bailing out rainwater from the gutters around the floorboards and lugging small carts of ammunition, food and supplies back and forth. She'd given herself an extra duty of checking her comrades' guns, when it became apparent she knew a lot more about the weapons than most of the men. They were slowly starting to warm to her.

It helped that young Toothless from the mess tent was circled through to her area, and he showed a keen interest in the way she tinkered with her own gun. She still had her scope and had been trying to figure out a way to attach it to the basic mumbler rifle. At first, she'd experimented with leather straps, but wasn't confident it'd hold consistently. She'd been trying to test it, popping off shots at a hunk of metal out in no-man's land, when Toothless asked her exactly how she knew how accurate it was. Impressed by her thorough answer, he offered to fashion her a metal frame, by bolting something into the mumbler's wooden casing.

Soon, Oksy had half a dozen men willing to talk to her, giving her (generally unsolicited) advice on everything from storing oatcakes to filleting goblins, while they lined up to hand over their rifles and see what she could do to fine-tune them. In the last week, with a broken coin for a screwdriver and a little pot of oil, she'd probably improved the calibration of about forty rifles, so they'd be easier to aim and less likely to jam. She'd even found a mess of large insect eggs in one gun barrel, which she flushed out rather than investigate the contents of; it could've cost the owner's life if he'd fired it and the shot was skewed. It could've cost more than that if those eggs hatched in the trench and spawned into sick-worms or mud-spiders.

The men fell into easy conversation with Oksy, shifting from regular jocular banter to occasional discussions of home, what people did before, the food and drink and activities they missed most. Oksy preferred to listen than talk, diverting questions with a lifted eyebrow or slight smile, or otherwise shared things she knew about how guns worked, or local wildlife, or phases of the moon. The people she'd left behind, her family and those apparent comforts, had no place here, and she worked to keep it that way.

The art of sharpshooting was Toothless's favourite subject, and her fond accounts of Major Heskeph's training never failed to brighten his eyes. The men went quiet and focused hard whenever she had a tip to offer about how better to hold a gun, track a target or ensure a kill.

"You gotta be one of the most deadly people we got," Toothless decided one evening, with a pot of beans bubbling over his little gas stove, a wonderful invention that improved all their lives. "Reckon you could kill a man without him ever knowing what hit him."

"That's generally the idea," Oksy agreed. "Anyone I can so much as see, if I've got the right rifle, I can take them down."

"We talking just men?" another soldier asked: Rogol, a bulky man with dark hair and intense eyes. He sounded accusatory, and stared hard, but that was just his manner – he meant well.

"Most creatures," Oksy said. "I've got a pretty good knowledge of all sorts of weak spots. Giants, cirga, grekkels."

"What about mages?" Rogol demanded, and she couldn't help smiling. There were six guys gathered around the beans and everyone awaited her answer raptly. It was the question she'd been torturing herself with, and a relief to hear others air the possibility.

She leant back. "A mage with a bullet coming at him would have a hard time acting fast enough to stop it. A parser might protect himself, if he had enough warning, but not an earth-minder."

"So all you'd have to do is get a line of sight on him," Rogol concluded, sounding more angry than impressed. "We just gotta get you a view of this fucker we been hiding from?"

Oksy liked the vote of confidence, but her eyes fell to her improvised mumbler, propped up against the dugout entrance. "If I had the right gun. Mumbler's good for a couple hundred metres, max, but I couldn't guarantee a hit like I could with something more powerful. With a properly rifled barrel, then yeah, I could hit anything in sight."

Rogol nodded along, like suddenly he knew all about this, and from the weight of his brow it had been taxing him for a while. "And we're sitting stirring beans waiting for the sky to fall on us. When we got a Bly-blessed sniper right here."

"In fairness, we'd have to find the mage first, anyway." Oksy recalled Wayflower's words: when Hold had died, they'd somehow lost another squad too. "I'm not sure our brigade's got any seasoned scouts left to locate him right now. But I'm pretty sure the dirt-minder's in one of two places, either the church or the silo. I could confirm that myself too, with a little reconnaissance. And we have a parser someone in our ranks, whoever stopped that building falling on us – with his help I'd be safe enough out there."

"Huh." Rogol stood, shaking his head like he was disappointed at the world in general, then stomped out of the dugout.

"Where you going?" Toothless cried. "What about your beans?"

"Gonna have a word," Rogol called back. His determination fired up the others to follow, abandoning the pot and Oksy. She smiled again. They were likely about to inspire Caracker's ire, but if she had others finally seeing things from her perspective, maybe they could get her point across where she couldn't. She leaned over and scooped up a spoonful of beans.

This wasn't so bad. Maybe it could be like Laine's Brigade after all. She hadn't been there long but the men had accepted her fraternally, like a sister they wanted to protect. Her sergeant had laid a man on his arse for trying to grab her. These boys were getting there, too.

They returned after twenty minutes looking sheepish and explained their requests had been denied: no one was sending Oksy out on what Captain Caracker called "a suicide mission". They'd argued back, receiving an earful in return, hence the downturned faces, and Toothless said it seemed Caracker *was* interested, just didn't like being told what to do. He'd think about it. On that tenuously positive note, they settled into their cooling beans with merry thoughts of triumph, and the night stretched out.

The next morning, a clamour came down through the trench that stirred everyone quickly out of their cots and into the chilly sunken walkways. Captain Caracker was thumping his way down the line, his voice audible long before he could be seen, issuing sharp orders and sending a wave of unsettled whispers on ahead.

The gist reached Oksy and her companions just as the ogre's broad shoulders came trudging around the bend in the trench: "Orders coming through to attack!"

Caracker paused at a distance when his eyes fell on Oksy, an especially grim look on his already grim face. It was always impressive to see him move through the trench; the passages were narrower than his shoulders and crowded with people but he made his way fluidly, with a lifetime's practice moving through a world too small for him. The men standing raggedly to attention blended into the mud walls as Caracker lurched directly for Oksy, bent to keep his head below the sight-line.

"Check your weapons, tighten your belts, lads, we're going over the top," he said, loud for all to hear but directed particularly at her. He stopped a few paces away, making Toothless cringe, and lowered his voice for Oksy. "Congratulations, you set off Colonel Wayflower."

"Sir?" Oksy exclaimed. "Me?"

"One mention, just one, that we had some idea where to find this mage, and how to stop them, and his mind went to the quickest way to ensure all our fates."

"You took the idea to him?"

"What'd you expect me to do? Getting your mates riled up, for a second you might've even had me believe it was a good idea. But the idea *he* got was that if we have a soldier confident of getting through to this mage's location, then maybe we try sending a whole brigade."

"One sniper –" Oksy started, but Caracker interrupted.

"Couldn't be trusted to do it alone. And he *really* didn't like the suggestion that our parser might help. You know who put up that shield for us? The one mage we've got? Wayflower's personal bloody bodyguard."

Oksy's memory flashed on that nervous officer who followed Wayflower everywhere.

"The one person he would *never* risk sending out," Caracker went on. "So here's your thanks for even suggesting it." He turned away, raising his voice louder for everyone to hear. "Full assault, the 203rd rises at dusk!" He moved on, making Oksy step back into the entrance of her dugout.

"That makes no sense!" Oksy cried. She went to follow Caracker, but he flashed her a knowing look, a sardonic smile. It said he had the same complaints, and they were useless.

The ogre swept on and the tension built through the trench, hundreds of nervous men now woken to awful news, likely to die today. Oksy found herself sitting back on her cot, staring into nothing, trying to recall all the lessons she'd learnt. Keep calm in the fight. Focus on breathing. Always account for wind. Only take the shots you can land. Then the lessons her father had taught her. Look for the unexpected. Observe and assess before you act. Do the right thing. Had she done anything right, if her choices had led her here? Joining the fight? Leaving home? Speaking up?

Her muddled thoughts were interrupted partly by other soldiers rushing in and out, shakily asking her to double-check their guns, and she absently did what she could.

Then they were ushered out along the line, pressed against the wall of the trench, wires cut above to let them through, everyone gripping guns tightly, ready to jump up into the slaughter. Oksy was pressed between Toothless and Rogol, and gave them each an encouraging smile whenever she caught the former's nervous eyes or the latter's wild stare. Rogol revived an oft-visited topic, one Oksy usually batted off: "How'd they let you in here anyway? Bloody disgrace, woman on the firing line."

"Should've been my brother," Oksy answered, still smiling but hearing that her voice was shaky. If they were about to die, she might as well let some of it out. "It was his name that came up, but he has weak legs. And a bad head for stress. I wasn't happy at home, so I took his place and no one cared."

"They didn't notice?" Toothless forced a laugh. "Bly, even if I was blind I'd smell it on you. Got a sweeter kind of sweat."

"Bullshit," Oksy laughed back. "I stink the same as anyone else." The recruiters *did* notice, though. They noticed on the boat over and in the training camp and in every station she'd had since. It was just that she was able to talk, lie and flirt her way through the process, mostly thanks to everyone being overstretched and too tired to care enough to turn her back. By the time she'd got to Farne, and was given a gun, Command decided they'd invested enough in her transport, and lost enough soldiers, that she might as well stay.

The rest of the day dragged out slowly, with terrible dread, but then the bell came all-too-quickly. A dull metal clang ran down the line, getting louder as other bells joined in, then shouting men answered the charge.

Oksy climbed up in the middle of hundreds of men, slipping on mud and tripping over broken rocks. They came up yelling, firing blind shots across no-man's land, at a set of ruined buildings behind the Drail's own trenches. The enemy didn't respond at once, taken at least partly by surprise, allowing the 203rd to get ten, maybe twenty metres across the rubble before meeting resistance. Then the buildings, and the top lip of the Drail trenches, lit up with a cascade of muzzle flashes, and the wall of Stanclif soldiers hit a wall of bullets, moving much faster and more ferociously than them.

Battle cries turned to screams of pain, charging soldiers tangling over falling men. Blood sprayed and parts of bodies and torn equipment burst up over the charge. There was an endless stretch to cross just to reach the Drail line, and every step cost dozens of lives.

Oksy was suddenly down, tripped on a rock, and Toothless ducked alongside her, a hand at her elbow to pull her back up. She pushed him off, shaking her head as she met his eyes, *no more!* He looked back as bullets rushed overhead, and one of their comrades flew past them, trailing blood.

"What are you –" Rogol half-turned in his run, and his jaw exploded as a shot tore through it. He dropped heavy, lifeless. A man running behind tripped over him and screamed incoherently before a bullet hit him, too.

Prone, Oksy hurried to get her rifle out from under her and propped it on a rock, aiming through the scope, between men's dashing legs. She picked out a muzzle flash and fired. Toothless huddled down next to her, flinching as a bullet hit the ground nearby.

"We can't make it," Toothless said, trembling. "There's no way."

"Onward you cowards!" Captain Caracker boomed furiously over the entire noise of battle. It rallied the force for a faster drive, even as more men fell by the second – but he was met by an equally loud shout from the other side. Not words in any language, but a screeching, mocking, ghastly sound that signalled one obvious thing. The mindless mage had arrived.

The gunfire stopped for a second, both sides shocked by the ferocity of the mage's voice, like a deranged, monstrous bird, though most of the 203rd kept running. Then the ground shook, the world quaking underneath them, and Oksy shifted onto her haunches to watch a great fissure open up just ahead of the charge. Chunks of ground rose and fell in angular, jagged shifts, like the working of some magnificent jaw, and the gap stretched wide, an abyss forming before them. The men at the front, moving too fast to stop, tumbled over the edge and screamed as they fell into the earth – they screamed long enough to show the hole was deep.

Caracker skidded up to the rift, looking down, a titan among his smaller soldiers. He snarled as he scanned ahead, appearing to consider jumping the gap, but it had to be ten metres wide, at least. He gave an order just before the firing started again: "Retreat!"

They were an army of men stood before a firing squad, though, and as the Stanclif boys backtracked the Drail opened up on them, hundreds of guns tearing through the ranks. Caracker twisted to the side and for the briefest second met Oksy's eye, seeing her lying down on the ground, far back. Then he caught a bullet in the shoulder, and went down to a knee as another hit his side. Oksy quickly picked out the muzzle flashes beyond him, jammed back her rifle bolt and fired. Again. She sent up divots of earth and sprays that could've been blood, firing along the Drail line, and the rifles quietened in that section, at least, as the enemy took cover. Soldiers were now falling around her less from being struck and more in the panic of trying to flop back over the trench line, into safety.

Caracker lurched back himself, shouting, "Get down, keep low, keep your arses!" He gave another pained roar and stumbled again, a shot catching him down the side of the leg. It came from above. He reeled towards it baring his teeth as if to punch back. Oksy followed the line of the shot over the trenches, up to a raised wall. A window in the half-broken remains of a house. A rifle poked out: a Drail soldier with a view of every man on the battlefield.

Oksy adjusted her aim and fired without hesitation. The enemy rifle jerked up, hit the window frame and fell out, the soldier dropping out of view. For a chill second, which she was surely imagining, the gunfire seemed to stop again, as if the world itself had been as surprised by her shot as they had been by the mage's cry. Men kept running though, urging each other on. The mindless mage, far off, kept laughing.

Caracker then thundered through the rest of the mess, at the rear of the line, still powerful and fast despite the shots he'd taken, and his presence pushed the rest of the men back even faster. They came rolling over Oksy's position, and after only a few more shots she was pulled back by Toothless, her comrade shouting, "Time to go!"

They tumbled over the edge of the trench together, landing hard on the planks and splashing in the mud, more boots slamming down around them. Oksy hurried to move out of the way of being trampled. She sat in a puddle breathing heavily, gun clutched hard to her chest, face wet with mud or blood, and tried to block out the chaotic sounds of death. Tried to unfocus her eyes and let go of what she'd seen.

Damn them, her thoughts raced.

Damn them for putting me here.

5

I say this all from a place of love. We trust you implicitly, and love you unconditionally, and you know I never doubted you believed what you said. But what is there to be gained, truthfully, now, in the face of all that is happening in the world, by continuing to punish yourself and others, over trivial fancies? I saw Juni and Alvina in the tavern and even they agreed with me; it may be hard to hear, but your own friends think you were too headstrong.

You are young, Okselle. Impulsive, imaginative. These are forgivable things. Everyone knows how young women can be and all you need to do to move on, really, is to accept that you might have been wrong. What do you say?

The overall mood in the trenches shifted after the failed charge, mostly more sombre, though Oksy realised the men were treating her with a kind of new reverence. She hadn't done much, but word had a habit of spreading, with her achievements on the battlefield inflated, as the men took courage in the stories. After all, it was easier to stomach this deadly situation if you believed there was a super-soldier on your side. But it left them careful and stilted, like they weren't sure if they should praise her or fear her. Not so comfortable as Laine's Brigade after all.

The soldiers kept questioning why the Drail hadn't come back at them straightaway, thinking any moment they'd be in for another battle, but Oksy thought it perfectly reasonable that they'd have a break. The Drail would've seen how easily the 203rd charge was decimated, and weren't foolish enough to attempt the same themselves. They were back to waiting each other out, testing the peripheries.

Until next time some fool officer got an idea for something glorious.

Skirmishes continued along the line, but the impassable rift the earth-minder had created spread the conflict further away, while Oksy was left in her relatively quiet position. She suspected the mage was still nearby though, still in their safe location on the other side. Almost two weeks passed, with no major conflicts in their vicinity.

The most danger Oksy found herself in was crawling up to repair wires or hiding from the ominous gaze of Caracker. He hadn't spoken to her since the battle, expect to snarl one-word commands, but she had an idea, from his distant scowling looks, that he was planning to. *Most* soldiers thought she'd done alright out there in the battle, but he'd seen her down on her belly, markedly not charging towards the enemy. Toothless, having taken cover down with her, had similarly grown worried about a reprisal, and made a special effort to avoid the ogre. But she had the added concern that the entire assault, really, could've been blamed on her interfering again.

Oksy was playing a game of rolling bones with her squad when Caracker finally shadowed the dugout entrance. He grunted, "With me, Price." In her moment's hesitation, where a dozen possibilities for reprimand and retribution popped up, he added, "Might as well bring your things."

Oksy flashed a look to her comrades, most of them with eyes down. Toothless met her eye but was frozen stiff, seemingly not daring to risk being noticed and called up with her. The ogre thumped off down the boards without waiting. Swearing, Oksy jumped up, scattering the dice game, and grabbed her pack and rifle. She was halfway out the dugout when she stopped, scrambled back in to grab her hairbrush off the bed and her weathered book about pirates.

"Come back, tell us what happens," Toothless whispered and she nodded, though they both knew that whatever this was, she probably wasn't coming back.

Caracker was near the turn in the trench already. Oksy skipped to catch up, noting his new slight limp. He'd been infirm for only a few days after the wounds he'd sustained, but despite an apparently speedy recovery he plainly had lasting troubles. Was it pain and shame he was finally about to take out on her?

"You can go home," he said, as she trotted up behind him, almost making her stop. She gave him a questioning look as he glanced at her. "They might even thank you for making things easier, the errant woman admitting she's had enough. You've served long enough for an honourable discharge, probably. They could parade you back in Vasseer."

He continued around another corner. Soldiers pressed into the walls to get out of his way and Oksy flashed them apologetic smiles as she followed, shifting to keep her pack tight to her shoulder. She noted Caracker's choice of words. *Can, could.* This wasn't a dismissal, exactly. She said, "I don't want to go home. I hoped the 203rd had come to accept me?"

Caracker snorted, unimpressed. "You've got a loving family to go back to, don't you? That doting father you always go on about. Your mates."

Oksy wasn't sure she'd mentioned her dad more than once in his presence. Had he been spying on her? "My father's not there to go back to. The rest of my family aren't so loving. I haven't got any friends."

"Yeah?" Caracker prompted. He didn't sound genuinely interested, marching ahead – now into the long south-channel, she noticed, away from the front – but Oksy decided to keep talking. If there was a chance of avoiding being turfed out to another uncertain company, she'd find it.

"My dad signed up when the war began. He was smart, brave. With him fighting for us, I thought we'd send the Drail all the way back up the Arrow in no time. He died in the very first conflict."

The ogre paused. "Halflight?" he checked, naming the first brutal battle of the war. Was there some grudging respect there?

Oksy nodded. "They told us he took a bullet to the head, but I learnt he was trampled by cirga. He tripped over before he got a chance to pull the trigger."

"Sounds like more reason your family need you."

"My family don't need me," Oksy told him firmly. "They don't *want* me."

Caracker eyed her carefully. There was definitely room for manoeuvre in his plans. He didn't patronise her with more false platitudes, but said, "Still better than here, isn't it? *You* don't have to stay."

"But I'm good at this," Oksy said. "This is what's important right now, isn't it? The whole world's future depends on what we do out here. If you'll just let me do *more.*"

"Aye. Figures you'd actually believe that, I suppose." He started walking again, big boots sloshing muddy water over cracked boards. He was going faster, taking them towards the rear of the battlements, and Oksy raced to catch up. He went on, "I've had another word with Colonel Wayflower. Had a word with a few others, too, seeing as he's learnt nothing from all the bloody-handed mistakes he's made."

Oksy raised an eyebrow. In certain circles, a statement like that would be enough to cost an officer his position, if not more.

"The Drail could strike at any time with that mindless prick of theirs, and Command know it. Wayflower's holding back. Waiting for the Drail to expose the bastard, withdrawing protection from his own bloody mage. And meantime he keeps petitioning General Macwest to send us some artillery or some other miracle cure for safely taking out the enemy from a distance."

"*I* could take out –" Oksy started, but Caracker flapped a hand at her to shut up. He came to a crossroads and paused, looking one way then another. Oksy knew that straight-on led to Barner's Field, mostly used for supply vehicles. To the left, a snaking route ran towards the eastern defences, as far as Fort Gawl, and to the right a network of tunnels served the ruins of the town of Luge. Oksy held in the urge to ask if he needed directions.

After a moment, the ogre moved right. Luge. It was where they were likely to meet Command, in the relative safety of burnt-out buildings. Oksy dug her heels in as Caracker went on a few paces.

He turned back and demanded, "What?"

"I'm a good sniper, sir. I might not be what you're used to, and might have made a few people upset, but I have value here. Whatever you think of me, when we charged, I *did* –"

"By Bly, *stop,*" Caracker growled wearily. "I don't need to hear it all again. We gotta meet someone – maybe for once just keep quiet until we've seen what they can do for us."

He continued walking, weaving his huge frame between the tight wooden supports. Oksy hesitantly followed, unsure now where this was going. Not to Wayflower himself, it seemed. To something more hopeful?

Broken stone walls started to rise over them, the sad shell of another town that had been fought through before the trenches were dug in. Caracker carefully picked his way through the less populated trenches and finally nodded satisfaction. Oksy looked past him to where the trench tunnelled into an old cellar, through a hole in a brick wall. As Caracker continued, he said, "Wayflower's requests were finally answered in the form of the fucking thing I told him we had all along. Command's sent us a scouting squad and they're confident they know where the mage is."

Oksy blew air through gritted teeth. So someone else was here to do her job. To take her chance to prove herself.

"I suggested to Wayflower that you join them, but you can imagine his response," Caracker went on, ducking into the brick tunnel. "He tried to blame the failed charge on you, seeing as how –" The ogre let out an angry huff, not even able to finish repeating such claims. "Doesn't matter. I went around him." He stopped before a thick oak door that barely reached his shoulders, massive hand on the handle. He said, "He's extra bitter now anyway, thinking the nature of the help Command sent is an insult and all. Ever heard of Tenacious Tate?"

Oksy shook her head.

"Hero of the Battle of the Basin, among a few other things." Caracker pushed the door open. A dark chamber awaited, barely lit. "In."

Oksy walked past, giving him a suspicious look, into a brickwork cellar left to waste, sideboards and tables thick with dust, vaulted ceiling cracked. There were four figures inside, all in light infantry uniform: scouting leathers, thinner and more mobile than most soldiers had. One pair were perched on a table, boots up on the bench: a hard-faced, lean-muscled woman with messy dark hair and a strikingly pretty companion with shining blonde hair in a long ponytail over one shoulder. The other pair were closer, standing towards the centre of the room, a softer-featured woman with sandy hair and a woman with a stiff, stern-lined face and a captain's cap.

Four female scouts.

The room was still as they took in Oksy and she took in them. The pretty one winked with a smile that belonged in a dance hall or at a cocktail party – nowhere near this war. Oksy caught herself, realising she was reacting to the sight of a woman soldier like the men did. It was weird to see. The impression was balanced, however, by the hard-looking one folding her arms, scowling and appearing every inch as tough as any soldier Oksy had known.

"Captain Tate." Caracker crouched his way into the cellar and stooped over them all. "This is Private Price. Saved my life and a lot of others at Jaggo Point."

Oksy flashed him a look. That's how he saw it? But that meant –

"You take her off my hands, I'll consider it a debt part paid," he went on. "Let her get hurt and I'll find you."

Tate, the stern officer, the only one here who looked old enough to have finished any kind of formal training, barely acknowledged the ogre in the room, eyes sharply on Oksy. She said, "Price. You're a trained sharpshooter?" She gave the rifle in Oksy's hand a sceptical look.

Oksy almost laughed, embarrassment rising up. She kept it down and said, "Yes, ma'am. Put a Long 0.48 or better in my hands and I can hit anything in a mile with almost perfect accuracy." She lifted the mumbler demonstratively. "I'm good up to two hundred metres with this."

Tate's lip quirked, just a flicker but it was something. Impressed or merely amused, it didn't matter. The woman next to her asked, "What's better than a Long 0.48?"

She was the hardest to read of the four, Oksy realised – possibly the youngest, not obviously commanding, tough or beautiful, but ordinary, even in the frank way she asked the question. A long gun case hung off her shoulder. Oksy replied with a question of her own, "You're a sniper, too?"

"Trained by Major Heskeph," the woman said.

"At Killen's Estate? I was there two months ago."

"Four." The woman pointed to herself, and Tate gave her a questioning look. The sniper shrugged. "Probably knows what she's doing."

"Let her prove it," the hard-faced one said, harder to impress. Addressing Oksy, she continued, "These prats want us to hunt a mage. Someone gave them the idea that's a thing regular scouts are good for."

"We are not regular scouts," Tate said, firm enough to cow the tough girl. "Our sharpshooters especially. Private Price, we had Boot Squad earmarked for this job. I intended to send Wild Wish with Loose and Rue, before Captain Caracker reached out. You can serve as a spotter as well as a sniper?"

Oksy's heart sank a little at the immediate degrading. She scanned the young sniper again, uneasy at the thought of having another possibly inexperienced superior. But she caught a look of warning in Caracker's eye. This wasn't a time to complain. She said, quietly, "Of course."

"Do you have any objection to leaving your current command?"

Oksy frowned at Caracker again and the ogre smiled his irregular grin, not so ugly now it appeared genuinely happy. How long had he been planning this? How above-board was it, given he'd gone against Wayflower? How was Oksy suddenly in a room with female soldiers, being *asked* what she wanted to do? She said, "Ma'am, I would be honoured to join you and doubly honoured to have a shot at this mage."

"Good," Tate said, and turned to the table where the other two women stood, "because we're taking care of it today. You've been in this theatre a while, give us your thoughts." Oksy and the sniper went with her to the table. The room shook with Caracker's footsteps as he came up behind, towering over their shoulders. The scouts pressed in close together to look at a map, a disappointingly amateur scrawl of uneven charcoal boxes and lines. It looked like a children's drawing.

"This is Wild's work so far," Tate said, nodding to the sniper, who gave a gentle finger-wave. "We're here, front line's here. Two clusters of buildings nearby, this one the bank where you spotted the land kraken." Oksy's ears pricked at that. It sounded like she giving her credit for the find, not accusing her? The captain went quickly on and in a few short minutes Oksy understood that however crude the drawing, and however unlikely these women's appearances, they knew the lay of the land well, and had picked out the same secure sites where the mage might be hiding which she would have. Hard-faced Rue said their first choice was the "fuck-off big metal silo" they thought would be hard to penetrate.

"It's the church," Oksy decided on the spot, that final comment securing it for her. Caracker huffed, a second's disappointment that she might say something to create a bad impression, but she tapped the map and quickly elaborated. "He's an earth-minder, they're less keen on surrounding themselves with metal. Industrial materials are less predictable or malleable for the mindless. He'll prefer something more natural."

There was a moment's silence as everyone stared at Oksy. Maybe Caracker was right to be cautious; it hadn't taken long for her to blurt out something with authority to total strangers. But if this was to be worth it, it had to be different . . .

Tate said, "Church it is, then. Settle up here and you can set out soon as you can."

With that surprise, Oksy found herself without a voice for a second. Warmth spread up through her. She cleared her throat and said, "I'm good to go now. I've been waiting for this chance."

6

Write to me, admit that you were mistaken, apologise to Mr Patterswald and his wife, and I will take care of the rest. We all know it was just a misunderstanding, the fancy of your rich imagination. He is a good person, sure to be forgiving, and the rumours you started really were quite unfair. How you expected anyone to believe such things of him, I do not know. And did you even consider the harm it would do to your own family's reputation?

But we shall not get into it again, shall we?

Better that you simply put it behind all of us. Come back from that awful war, clear his name and ours alike. Our door remains ever open to you. This is where you belong.

Your loving mother,

Angen

She'd made it.

The church sat ahead, a stone tower with a small annex jutting out to its right. Lying on her front, pressed close to the sniper Wild Wish, Oksy peered through her scope, whispering, "It's a celebrant tower, essentially one hollowed-out cylinder. Walkways all around the centre going up to a great bell at the top. The hall at the side is usually just for storage."

Oksy lowered the scope to see her fellow sniper. Wish had an eyebrow raised, suggesting she was unsure what to do with that information.

"It means the main services, and facilities, are all centred under that bell," Oksy went on, indicating the great brass dome that hung from an open wooden structure at the top of the tower. The silhouettes of two soldiers with long rifles stood up there, occasionally pacing about. It was a great vantage point, likely providing a view all the way back to the front line, and it had taken a lot of care for the snipers to crawl up this ridge without being seen.

Wish shuffled in the foliage, shoulder brushing against Oksy, and Oksy shifted to give her space. She settled again, their shoulders touching, and Oksy realised she was already more comfortable with this woman than she'd ever been with Hold.

The women had all been welcoming, with Loose whispering on parting, "When you get back you're telling me how you keep your hair that clean."

She had to be humouring Oksy, only trying to be friendly, given that her own hair was immaculate and Oksy's really wasn't, but it was nice all the same. And of them all, Wild Wish in particular felt like someone Oksy could work with. She had trained under Heskeph, just like her. That guaranteed a certain degree of skill. She also had an endearing shyness about her. It hadn't escaped Oksy's attention how Wish had looked at the beautiful blonde, and hugged her when they were on the way out of Luge. When they had set out together and Oksy asked if Wish liked girls, the sniper had shrugged, abashed. Through the journey up here, Wish had then made suggestions, not commands, waiting for Oksy's take on each direction they took. For once, Oksy felt like she wasn't in competition, even if she had a very personal need to prove herself.

"So if I shoot one of those guards and he falls down the middle," Wild Wish said, looking through her rifle scope, "that'll alert everyone and maybe send them running out. Or at least get them popping heads in windows to give me a few more shots."

Oksy considered this. The church tower only had a couple of very thin windows, the structure designed to double as a battlement. They weren't going to be able to shoot anyone inside with much ease. She said, "They designed these towers to be deliberately top-heavy. The over-sized bells were lifted afterwards, to deliberately remind the celebrants of the power of their gods above. Generally structurally sound, but emphasising the fragility of the congregation."

"Yeah," Wild Wish agreed, "it does look kind of stupid."

"I mean to say," Oksy went on, "that big-arse bell up there would cause a lot of damage coming down. It's only hanging by a small chain."

Wish took another look. "That *is* a small chain."

"It'd knock through the guard platforms, hit some of the upper prayer structures, maybe roll off and catch a wall. If we're lucky it could take down the whole church. I'm surprised they didn't remove the bell, to be honest – it's a liability in wartime."

Wish gave her another curious glance. "How do you remove a bell like that?"

"They'd usually have a system of cranes. Maybe they never had time, or wanted to give the appearance that the building was unoccupied. But what do you think? We sever that bell and it might crush the mage without a fight. Though I don't know how we'd verify the kill then."

"Easy. We'd ask ourselves, *did that look likely to kill a mage or not?* But you don't think a mindless mage could repel a giant falling bell?"

"That's not how it works," Oksy said, stifling a small laugh at Wish's earnest phrasing. The sniper's face remained deadpan, so Oksy explained, "The mindless have to be touching something to manipulate it. He wouldn't have time to stop the bell if it hit him at speed. If it missed and he got caught in the rubble, yes, he might get clear, but I think this can work."

"Take down a building with one shot. It's ambitious." Wild Wish chewed a lip as she studied the bell. She didn't sound too sure, and Oksy felt a familiar anxiety growing in her. Whether or not to speak.

She rushed the words out: "I can make that shot. I'm sure of it. If you want."

Wish looked from her then down to the rifle, face unreadable for a second. "I probably can, too." After another pause, she said, "Is it true you unleashed a land kraken?"

"Not exactly. My partner fired the shot that triggered it, and it wasn't *unleashed,* it just tore up the street and ate him. I managed to run clear of it and it settled back down pretty quickly. But Dagger Legion's command lost their cool and fled the building anyway. I could've shot half their officers dead if I had a gun. Instead, our guys got angry about it and threw me in the trenches."

"Oh?" Wild Wish sat back slightly, considering her own rifle at length. "And you want to take the lead this time?"

"I'm a good shot. I've barely had a chance to prove it. I came out here to make a difference, after my father – and after this *stupid* thing back home –" Oksy stopped, hearing herself rambling, with the collected weight of losing her dad, then losing everyone else back home, bubbling up. She needed this, to make up for it all. Almost to herself, she added quietly, "I can shoot well. I can do anything well. If people would just stop . . ."

Meeting Wish's eye again, she found the other sniper staring at her strangely. She held the gun out to Oksy and said, "I honestly don't care who does it. Seems important to you."

Oksy looked from the weapon back up to Wish's face, the other woman's brow raised encouragingly. She took a breath, hardly believing it. The Blood Scouts, she was quite sure, were people she could work with. Just as soon as they killed this mage. Oksy reached for the gun and positioned it carefully, picked out the chain supporting the bell. Wild Wish gave her the distance and wind, and Oksy adjusted the scope.

She took a breath, calming herself, and squeezed the trigger.

The gun reported with a loud clap, bucking against Oksy, but she held it tight and kept her eye on the bell as she slid the bolt for another shot. The great brass object was already falling, the chain severed, and as she looked over the scope it crashed down through the parapet. One soldier was thrown clear of the tower as the other fell into the mess of breaking wood along with the bell.

The noise was thunderous, the descent slow but unstoppable, as the bell smashed into the stone and disappeared inside. Cracks erupted over the stonework and the tower folded in on itself with great clangs announcing each heavy impact of the fall. Dust and debris exploded out of the lower windows just before the bell hit the base and the entire structure collapsed.

It took a full minute for the immense sound to stop echoing through the nearby ruins.

The dust slowly settled in a brown mist, the stonework giving a few final shifts as it came to rest, and then all was quiet. Whoever had been inside was surely crushed.

"That looked likely to kill everyone inside," Wish whispered. "Good shot."

Oksy nodded, amazed that it had worked. Movement in her periphery drew her attention off to the left, though, and she scoped a group of green-coat soldiers hurrying towards the ruined church from a distant position. Time to go. But Wish nudged her and nodded at the ruins, where Oksy saw the stonework shift. Something pushing up.

She swore just before the debris burst out, a slab of wall thrown twenty feet high, and a man launched out of the wreckage like a corpse animated from the grave. He landed on top of the fallen structure shaking out his long limbs, shredded greatcoat flapping about him, then he roared to the sky with a jackal's laughter. The mindless mage, darkened by dust, looked inhumanly feral, ferocious and invincible, and as his laughter dipped he hunched sharply forward, to scan the surrounding area.

Oksy targeted him, but the gun was shaking in her hands, the sight bouncing on and off his head. This was bad. She finally had a gun, finally had a chance, and couldn't aim. An alert mage was about the most dangerous thing the war had to offer and he was *hunting* for her.

"Cowards!" the mage screeched, hands swinging about like claws as he swung side to side. He crouched, driving his fingers into the stone, to send his magic into the earth.

"He's in the open," Wish said and Oksy nodded, but she still couldn't steady her sights. If she missed, giving away their position, the mage would be on them in a second.

She felt the presence of Wild Wish's hand before the touch itself, Wish hesitating over making contact. Oksy tensed, tightening her grip, not wanting to give the gun back. But the hand only rested on her shoulder, warm and gentle. Flatly reassuring. Oksy exhaled and relaxed into the rifle.

"The world will swallow you!" the mage screamed, shaking with rage, and the ground quaked under his command, spreading from the rubble under him in expanding circles, tossing up stone and brick with a bone-breaking pulse, quickly approaching their position. The approaching Drail soldiers stopped and began backing up in the reasonable fear that the mage might flatten friend and foe alike with this power.

Oksy breathed, hung onto the assurance of Wish's touch, stilled her hand and fired.

The maniac was thrown off his feet in a flurry of torn coat. The quaking stopped as he crumpled, and once more the world was quiet. Everything was still, no one moving near or far, and Oksy waited with dread for the coat to twitch, the monstrous man to rise up and attack again.

He didn't move, though, and didn't make a sound.

She had killed a mindless mage. A single action that would make more impact than all Wayflower's senseless assaults combined. She'd done it, had to be recognised now, had to move towards finally finding her place in this forsaken world.

Wild Wish, hand still on her shoulder, gave Oksy a slight squeeze, and said, quietly, "I guess you're a Blood Scout now. Welcome to the Empire's least-appreciated platoon."

Thanks for Reading!

Hello from me, the author, Phil Williams! I hope you enjoyed *Oksy, Come Home*, as a return to the world of the Rocc. If it's your first foray into the Blood Scouts, then do check out *However Many Must Die.* If you'd like to leave a review, please do so wherever you can online and tell other people about it. Every bit of extra notice helps.

There's more to come from the series, so watch out for news on my upcoming releases, but in the meantime if you've enjoyed the Blood Scouts so far, why not check out my other work? The Ordshaw series is fairly different, as contemporary fantasy thrillers, but you'll find similar unusual creatures, chaotic action, unstable characters and wild situations!

Also By Phil Williams

THE BLOOD SCOUTS SERIES
HOWEVER MANY MUST DIE
DROWN DEEP

ORDSHAW SERIES
The Sunken City Trilogy
UNDER ORDSHAW
BLUE ANGEL
THE VIOLENT FAE

Tova Noakes
THE CITY SCREAMS

The Ikiri Duology
KEPT FROM CAGES
GIVEN TO DARKNESS

Punk Witches
DYER STREET PUNK WITCHES

Shorts
THE ORDSHAW VIGNETTES VOL. 1

ESTALIA SERIES
WIXON'S DAY
BALFAIR'S CONFINEMENT
AFTAN WHISPERS

FAERGROWE SERIES
A MOST APOCALYPTIC CHRISTMAS